A Mother Goose Book

A Mother Goose Book

by joan walsh anglund

GULLIVER BOOKS

HARCOURT BRACE JOVANOVICH, PUBLISHERS

San Diego   New York   London

HBJ

Requests for permission to make copies of any part of the work should be mailed to:
Permissions Department,
Harcourt Brace Jovanovich, Publishers,
Orlando, Florida 32887.

Library of Congress Cataloging-in-Publication Data
A Mother Goose book.
A Mother Goose book/[illustrated] by Joan Walsh Anglund.
p.   cm.
"Gulliver books."
Summary: An illustrated collection of Mother Goose nursery rhymes,
including "Jack and Jill," "Pease Porridge Hot,"
and "Jack Be Nimble."
ISBN 0-15-200529-3
1. Nursery rhymes. 2. Children's poetry. [1. Nursery rhymes.]
I. Anglund, Joan Walsh, ill. II. Title.
PZ8.3.M85   1991
398.8 — dc20   90-4466

Printed in Singapore
First edition
A B C D E

With love for

Emily	Cecily
Thaddeus	Mathias
Aurora	Max
Jane	Molly
Carolyn	Sarah
Tori	Justin
Stephen	Julie
Mark	Jaclyn
Daniel	Jalena
Anna	Kaila

Little Bo-peep has lost her sheep,
And can't tell where to find them;
Leave them alone, and they'll come home,
And bring their tails behind them.

Rub-a-dub-dub,

Three men in a tub;

And who do you think they be?

The butcher, the baker,

The candlestick maker,

Turn 'em out, knaves all three!

Jack and Jill
went up the hill
To fetch a pail
of water;

Jack fell down
and broke his crown,
And Jill came
tumbling after.

The Queen of Hearts
She made some tarts,
All on a summer's day;
The Knave of Hearts
He stole the tarts
And took them clean away.

The King of Hearts
Called for the tarts,
And beat the Knave full sore;
The Knave of Hearts
Brought back the tarts,
And vowed he'd steal no more.

To market, to market,
to buy a fat pig,
Home again, home again,
jiggety-jig;

To market, to market,
to buy a fat hog,
Home again, home again,
jiggety-jog.

Pease porridge hot,
Pease porridge cold,
Pease porridge in the pot
Nine days old.

Some like it hot,
Some like it cold,
Some like it in the pot
Nine days old.

Little Tommy Tittlemouse
Lived in a little house;
He caught fishes
In other men's ditches.

Butterfly, Butterfly,
Whence do you come?
I know not, I ask not,
I never had home.

Butterfly, Butterfly,
Where do you go?
Where the sun shines
And where the buds are.

Ding, dong, bell,
Pussy's in the well.
Who put her in?
Little Johnny Green.
Who pulled her out?
Little Tommy Stout.

What a naughty boy was that,
To try to drown poor pussy cat,
Who never did him any harm,
And killed the mice in his father's barn.

This little pig went to market,
This little pig stayed at home,
This little pig had roast beef,
This little pig had none,
And this little pig cried, Wee! wee! wee!
All the way home.

Wee Willie Winkie
runs through the town,
Upstairs and downstairs
in his nightgown;
Rapping at the window,
crying through the lock,
Are the children all in bed,
for now it's eight o'clock?

Curly Locks, Curly Locks,
Wilt thou be mine?
Thou shalt not wash dishes
Nor yet feed the swine,
But sit on a cushion
And sew a fine seam,
And feed upon strawberries,
Sugar, and cream.

Daffy-down-dilly
　　is new come to town,
With a yellow petticoat,
　　and a green gown.

What is the news of the day,
Good neighbor, I pray?
They say the balloon
Is gone up to the moon!

Here am I,
　　Little Jumping Joan;
When nobody's with me
　　I'm all alone.

Mary had a little lamb,
Its fleece was white as snow;
And everywhere that Mary went
The lamb was sure to go.

It followed her to school one day,
That was against the rule;
It made the children laugh and play
To see a lamb at school.

Little Boy Blue,
Come blow your horn,
The sheep's in the meadow,
The cow's in the corn;

But where is the boy
Who looks after the sheep?
He's under a haystack,
Fast asleep.

Jerry Hall,
He is so small,
A rat could eat him,
Hat and all.

Jenny Wren last week was wed,
And built her nest in grandpa's shed;
Look in next week and you shall see
Two little eggs, and maybe three.

I sing, I sing
From morn 'til night,
From cares I'm free
And my heart is light.

Georgie Porgie, pudding and pie,

Kissed the girls and made them cry;

When the boys came out to play,

Georgie Porgie ran away.

Three little kittens they lost their mittens,

And they began to cry,

Oh, mother, dear, we sadly fear

That we have lost our mittens.

What! lost your mittens, you naughty kittens!

Then you shall have no pie.

Meow, meow, meow.

No, you shall have no pie.

The three little kittens they found their mittens,

And they began to cry,

Oh, mother dear, see here, see here,

For we have found our mittens.

Put on your mittens, you silly kittens,

And you shall have some pie.

Purr-r, purr-r, purr-r,

Oh, let us have some pie.

Cross-patch,
Draw the latch,
Sit by the fire and spin;
Take a cup
And drink it up,
Then call your neighbors in.

Tom, Tom, the piper's son,
Stole a pig and away he run;
The pig was eat,
And Tom was beat,
And Tom went howling down the street.

Ring-a-ring o' roses,
A pocket full of posies,
A-tishoo! A-tishoo!
We all fall down.

Jack be nimble,
Jack be quick,
Jack jump over
the candlestick.

Bobby Shafto's gone to sea,
Silver buckles at his knee;
He'll come back and marry me,
Bonny Bobby Shafto!

Bobby Shafto's fat and fair,
Combing down his yellow hair;
He's my love for evermore
Bonny Bobby Shafto!

There was an old woman
Lived under a hill,
And if she's not gone
She lives there still.

I'm glad the sky is painted blue,
And the earth is painted green,
With such a lot of nice fresh air
All sandwiched in between.

Simple Simon met a pieman,
Going to the fair;
Says Simple Simon to the pieman,
Let me taste your ware.

Says the pieman to Simple Simon,
Show me first your penny,
Says Simple Simon to the pieman,
Indeed, I have not any.

Old King Cole
Was a merry old soul,
And a merry old soul was he;
He called for his pipe,
And he called for his bowl,
And he called for his fiddlers three.

The Man in the Moon looked
    out of the moon,
Looked out of the moon
    and said,
'Tis time for all children
    on the earth
To think about getting to bed!

Come to the window,
My baby, with me,
And look at the stars
That shine on the sea!
There are two little stars
That play at bo-peep
With two little fish
Far down in the deep;
And two little frogs
Cry neap, neap, neap;
I see a dear baby that
should be asleep.